carlos, the dawn
is no longer beyond
our reach

carlos, the dawn is no longer beyond our reach

The prison journals
of **Tomas Borge**
remembering Carlos Fonseca,
founder of the FSLN.

New Star Books
Vancouver, Canada

The chronology was translated by Marie Lorenzo. The manuscript was edited by Marie Lorenzo and Lynda Yanz. Photos by Margaret Randall, Deborah Barndt, and thank you to Colin McAdam. Historical research by David Kidd. Cover by Stuart Morris.

Canadian Cataloguing in Publication Data

Borge, Tomas, 1930-
    Carlos, the dawn is no longer beyond our reach

Translation of: Carlos, el amanecer ya no es una tentacion.
ISBN 0-919573-24-X (bound). — ISBN
    0-919573-25-8 (pbk.)

1. Fonseca Amador, Carlos - Chronology.
2. Frente Sandinista de Liberacion Nacional -
History - Chronology. 3. Nicaragua - History -
1937-1979 - Chronology. I. Title.
F1527.F66B6713 1984   972.85'052'0924   C84-091435-0

1   2   3   4   5   88   87   86   85   84

New Star Books Ltd.
2504 York Avenue
Vancouver, B.C. V6K 1E3

PRINTED AND BOUND IN CANADA

translator's introduction

Tomas Borge Martinez is the "elder brother" of the Nicaraguan revolution, the extraordinary survivor of more than twenty years of struggle. He is the only one left of the trio — Carlos Fonseca, Silvio Mayorga and himself — that founded the Sandinista National Liberation Front (FSLN), and began the long, hard, terrible, crazy and self-sacrificing, almost unimaginable and historic task of changing the face of their homeland. He is currently one of the nine members of the FSLN's National Directorate and Minister of the Interior in Nicaragua's National Reconstruction Government. He is the head of State Security, the police, the forces of order — and the enemies of the Nicaraguan revolution never tire of portraying him as a tyrant or dictator.

Yet Tomas is someone radiating love, the initiator of poetry workshops among the country's soldiers. Keeper of "law and order," he is also the major spokesperson for the unique generosity of this revolution. Having suffered imprisonment as few have suffered it — long periods of isolation, severe torture — he "took revenge" on his torturer by pardoning him. For three years after the Sandinista victory, Tomas lived in a large house in the

5

elegant residential suburb of Las Colinas, south of the city of Managua. Suddenly he, along with his wife Josephine, his children and his extended family, all moved into the working class neighborhood of Bello Horizonte, farther into the capital. Nicaraguans were not surprised.

Tomas' *Carlos, The Dawn Is No Longer Beyond Our Reach* is a tribute to Carlos Fonseca, the leader of the FSLN until his death in 1976, written while Tomas was in prison and begun when he received the news of the death, in combat, of his old friend and comrade. No one is better equipped to write about Fonseca than Tomas Borge. Tomas knew and was close to Carlos Fonseca from adolescence, a friendship that was to acquire historic dimensions and transcend the latter's death.

What these notes may lack in accuracy (due to the limitations of writing in prison), they make up for in poetry, passion and that truth which is so much more than the sum total of its parts. It offers a unique glimpse of the Nicaraguan struggle, from the perspective of the FSLN. Alive in its pages is the continuity from the veteran Sandinistas (survivors of the 1927-1934 war) to those who were finally able to draw on Sandino's legacy and build the revolutionary organization capable of toppling the dictatorship; and there is a sense of how that was done — the search, the patience, the tenacity, the singleness of purpose, the audacity, and most of all, the faith. The faith that what was being done was inevitable and necessary. And the faith — even when in all of Nicaragua the FSLN numbered a dozen or two — that they would win. The "they" was collective: each man and woman, individually, easily imagined he or she might not live to see victory. Through those years, what was being forged was the consciousness of the collective, without ever losing sight of each individual's uniqueness and worth.

These are poetic pages — indeed this is one of the great poems to have emerged from the Nicaraguan struggle — but they are not romantic, nor lacking in critical insight.

6

As much attention is given to the FSLN's fumbling, its growing pains, its errors and reassessments, as is given to its great heroisms.

The style, the flow of words and ideas, the frequent jumps from memory to memory may confuse the reader who is expecting a straightforward chronology. Though it appears to be set out as a chronology, in fact the dated sections are inserted to provide a backdrop, like the set for a play, to the unfolding drama that is the vision of Carlos Fonseca as seen and lived through the eyes of Tomas Borge. It is a style unique to Latin American literature, and it requires a certain suspension of our usual expectations about consistency of time and space, in order to let the poetry, the sentiments, the reality and the vision form a total impression. For the English language edition we have included a chronology of Carlos Fonseca's life to help set the context.

Toward the end of the poem we have the lines which have become such a representative part of the Nicaraguan struggle that they now form part of the FSLN anthem: "...the dawn is no longer beyond our reach...tomorrow, one day, soon, an as-yet-unknown sun will shine on that earth our heroes and martyrs promised us. An earth with rushing rivers of milk and honey, where all human beings will be as brothers and sisters."

The Sandinista revolution is now five years old, and eight years have passed since these lines were spoken in a military court in Managua by a man, Tomas Borge, far more interested in projecting his people's courage and purpose than in surviving in his human flesh. Reading these lines today, it is important that we not lose sight of the circumstances in which they were originally uttered.

Margaret Randall
Albuquerque, N.M.
Spring, 1984

carlos, the dawn
is no longer beyond
our reach

Carlos Fonseca

introduction

The writer of these lines is as much an author as Garcia Marquez is a refrigerator salesman. These lines, though, have a different merit: they were written almost entirely in prison, possessed by the god of fury and the devil of tenderness.

I dedicate this humble effort to my brother Modesto, the most modest, stubborn, fraternal and honest guerrilla leader that the Sandinista National Liberation Front ever produced. And to our combatants in the mountains who live, sing and struggle through every ambush, each new exhaustion, on the edge of Carlos Fonseca's sun and dreams.

i

That explosion of rhymed poems, learning to dance, crossing the street beneath a lantern of stares, exploring peasant homes in search of the secret of fresh cheese and a buck in a .22 rifle sight, sharing the joys and tensions of Winnetou* with my friends; writing careful and effusive letters only to discover at the last minute that Vilma was Anibal's girlfriend. And then there was Guillermo. We envied him the personal magnetism in his eyes, his confidence: he wouldn't masturbate with the group, and all the girls would wave at him as he walked down the street.

It was the time of Teresita, of monumental blemishes, black eyes, incorrigible diction, of shivers, perhaps whispers; of Bolivar's anniversaries. "If there is anyone

---

* Native American character in the series of "western" novels by German writer Karl May. "Old Shatterhand and Winnetou expressed, in my judgement, the best qualities human beings ought to have...a tremendous respect, almost a fanatical respect, for personal loyalty, for courage, for generosity, for disregarding danger, and for human solidarity." Interview with Tomas Borge in *Risking a Somersault in the Air: Conversations With Nicaraguan Poets* by Margaret Randall, Solidarity Press, 1984.

here who is freedom's enemy, let the earth swallow him up; Bolivar will be back with whip in hand to expel him from the temple!" Our temple was someone's backyard with a few old chairs, decrepit and prone to surprises.

And not too much later: *Spartacus*, the weekly that sold like fresh bread in which we wrote vaguely but fervently of Sandino.

I don't know if it was Marina's black eyes or the fact that she sang softly and persistently: all of a sudden there was awkwardness, cold chills, magic. Maybe it was because the river sounded so close to her quivering knees, or because she was the first girl to smell of night and sweat who looked me in the eyes; the fact was, I was sad and evasive.

I admit, even for me — star pitcher in a tribe of kids recently sporting their new men's voices — it was hard to be sad. On Sundays, impossible. At night it was different, for then I read Flaubert, Becquer and Karl May.

When I became *antisomocista*, I read Alberto Masferrer and they threw me in jail. And I stopped being sad, adolescent and going to the parades to talk to the girls.

nineteen thirty-four

On February 21, 1934, with the murder of our national hero Augusto Cesar Sandino — and hundreds of other patriots — U.S. imperialism and our country's Liberal-Conservative oligarchy brutally beat down our popular and patriotic movements. From that moment on, our people are not able to find a fighting alternative. In the country, no direction exists, neither organization nor revolutionary consciousness. Political activity was left to the traditional parties in Nicaragua.

Tomas Borge, now Minister of the Interior for Nicaragua

ii

It was in this instant that Carlos Fonseca appeared. He came to us with his blue eyes, brusque and myopic. He came whole, serious, cordial, with his white pegged-pants and his expansive gestures. At the Institute: 100 per cent in algebra, in French and in everything else. In the street: his quick long legs — he was a mailman to help his mother, Justina — without stopping to take in the subtle glances the recipients gave to the sender's name and address. Always a book under his arm between acts.

The first meetings were in Lala's backyard, under the shade of birds, *jocote* and orange trees. We discovered Tomas Moro, John Steinbeck and later Marx and Engels hidden in the poet Samuel Meza's dusty old bookstore. Through that dark night Lenin was no more than an inaccessible bibliographic reference.

From the beginning, without meaning to, Carlos led our incipient efforts, through those afternoons interrupted by gourds filled with milk and *pinol*, trying to grasp something other than what was fed us in the classroom, in the newspapers, at church.

A couple of years earlier he had wanted to be a saint — as he revealed to me much later in that inevitable sharing of secrets. We saw him take his first communion at a pale ceremony of poor children with their white candles adorned with the gold paper his mother kept in a long wooden box where for years she saved the ever more sonorous and irreproachable relics of her son.

When he didn't want to be a saint anymore — but was one anyway — he and Chico Buitrago founded *Segovia*, a magazine of strange symbols and prophetic editorials.

iii

When we got to the university, he cried with that ferocity that sometimes laces sorrow. Blue eyes weeping, and who wouldn't? The university was a roof, a few walls and indifferent halls, obscene, with no recognizable nostalgias and stinking of dissected stray dogs: the ebbtide.

Carlos made himself ant, hammer, typist and — from that moment on — everlasting. He painted subversive slogans from wall to wall and handed out student and Party* papers from door to door. Almost immediately *El Universitario* (The University Student) appeared, with large headlines and in two colors. We published statistics without metaphor: 250,000 children without schools and without teachers; only 5 per cent taxation to the mining companies on the gold they exported and no taxation on the agriculture and mining machinery, automobiles,

---

* Refers to the *Partido Socialista Nicaraguense* (PSN) which Fonseca joined in July 1955. "From 1959 to 1962, we still maintained the illusion that it was possible to bring about change through the peaceful means proposed by the PSN leadership." (Carlos Fonseca, *Zero Hour*)

electrical appliances, etcetera they imported. Numbers:
our country pays foreign investors to exploit our sub-soil
so they can take our gold. And we're left with the cough.

iv

Around then we were semi-recruited by the Socialist Party, and Carlos led the first Marxist cell of Nicaraguan university students: Silvio Mayorga* was one of its three members. A guy from Leon who lived in Mexico (we never knew whether he was a Marxist or a cowboy) was sent from the Socialist Party to have discussions with us.

"Sandino," Carlos said on one occasion, "is a path. It would be superficial to reduce him to a category or to one more date on the yearly calendar of activities. I think it is important to study his thought."

The guy from Leon got scared and answered more less as follows:

"A path? That's poetry! Don't forget what a suspect hero certain bourgeois ideologues have made of that guerrilla. Sandino fought against foreign occupation, not against imperialism. He wasn't a Zapata...I mean, he didn't deal with the question of the land."

Carlos expressed his doubts when faced with these arguments. He began to investigate Sandino's thought

---

* Close friend, comrade and joint founder of the FSLN with Tomas Borge and Carlos Fonseca.

Augusto C. Sandino

more thoroughly. I remember the joy and severity of his violent outburst when he came across the book *El calvario de las segovias* (The Calvary of the Segovias) in which the author attempts to belittle our immortal hero.* That was the first biographic reference before we found *Sandino: o la tragedia de un pueblo* (Sandino: or a people's tragedy) by the honest historian Sofias Salvatierra; a book by a Spaniard with a long name impossible to remember; Calderon Ramirez' work; and, finally, Selser's books.† With precision and diligence, Carlos took notes, jotting down phrases from Sandino's rich correspondence. In those notes *Ideario Sandinista* (Sandinista Ideology), handbook of basic concepts that circulates among FSLN militants, was conceived.

* A distortion of Sandino's life commissioned by Somoza.

† Gregorio Selser, Argentinian. "It is interesting to note that a person who has never breathed the air of Nicaragua is the one who until now has elaborated the most complete review of the facts concerning the epic of Sandino." (Carlos Fonseca, *Long Live Sandino*)

nineteen fifty-six

Our national hero Rigoberto Lopez Perez settles accounts with the tyrant Anastasio Somoza Garcia on September 21, "so Nicaragua may become once more (or for the first time) a free country, with neither stain nor indignity."

V

Carlos travelled to Moscow in 1957 as the Socialist Party delegate to the World Youth Congress. From a European city — Prague — he wrote with moving loyalty to his mother. Even though my memory is not great, I still remember the content of one of those tender messages:

"I'm almost happy, mama: among joyful young people; new words; great, friendly and beautiful cities; we call each other comrade, though I would like to call my friends brother and sister. I'm *almost* happy, I say, because you are not at my side to hug and share these moments of clarity and astonishment."

When he returned to Nicaragua, he wrote *Un Nicaraguense en Moscu* (A Nicaraguan in Moscow) in which he tells of his experiences with his usual directness and in a clean, accessible language.

At the university, he is the permanent delegate of the pre-FSLN clandestine groupings; he is leader of the student assemblies and university organizations. He organizes the first national students' strike, including primary students, with class stoppages rotating every 48 hours. "Instructions from Moscow" was what *Nove-*

dades* called it. The strike was to secure the release of several professors and a student who had been unjustly sentenced by a military court.

He was always agitating; in the neighborhoods of Leon he was a leader as well. He organized people's committees to demand better living conditions and deal with other concerns which, inevitably, soon became political demands.

* Somoza-controlled newspaper.

nineteen fifty-eight

Ramon Raudales, veteran Sandinista, wields his guerrilla rifle again and dies fighting the National Guard.

vi

In 1957* Carlos founded New Nicaragua, a movement born lame and inhibited. Nonetheless, it represented the first steps of a group of young people who tried to march toward the sun through the subterranean channels of the underground.

The movement took the initiative of establishing a publishing house by the same name; Selser's works and a few revolutionary tracts came off its presses.

That effort, so difficult when it was launched, was exceptionally important historically if we consider the ideological and cultural desert we lived in. The Nicaraguan people have been prisoners behind a wall built with patriarchal and oligarchic patience from the time of our independence from Spain, and that wall was enforced by the founder of the Somoza dynasty with gross words, bayonet-points and legal measures. Our isolation has been so crude and complete that when the author of these lines got to the university and met groups of students — who later became university presidents and bankers — he

---

* The actual year of the formation of *Movimiento Nueva Nicaragua* was 1961.

believed, as they all did, that Haya de la Torre* was a Marxist revolutionary and that there was no working-class party in Nicaragua.

Of course, no one cared about the students in those days, no one offered a miserable cube of sugar to attract them. It wasn't until four years later that the Socialist Party became aware of the students' existence, around the time Carlos entered the university. Later he was to say, with just cause, that the current revolutionary process in Nicaragua emerged more from embarrassment than from consciousness.

The victory of armed struggle in Cuba, more than just delighting our hearts, was the parting of innumerable curtains, an explosion that showed the naive and boring dogmas of those times for what they really were. The Cuban revolution sent a terrifying chill running through America's ruling classes and shattered the suddenly outmoded relics with which we'd begun to adorn our political altars. For us, Fidel was the resurrection of Sandino, the answer to our doubts, the justification for our heretical dreams of just a few hours before.

* Haya de la Torre was a Peruvian populist leader and social democrat.

nineteen fifty-nine

The victory of armed struggle in Cuba sparks the enthusiasm of the Nicaraguan people and gives impetus to our struggle against the dictator.

A group of men land by plane at Olama y Mollejones. Several dozen, heavily armed, are captured by the National Guard. Ex-military captains Victor Manuel Rivas and Napoleon Ubilla, who participate in the expedition, are killed.

In June, the Rigoberto Lopez Perez guerrilla column, which in its planning stage had the support of Ernesto "Che" Guevara, is brutally attacked at El Chaparral — on the border between Nicaragua and Honduras — by the armies of both countries. Several Nicaraguans and Cubans die. Carlos Fonseca is badly wounded.

To protest the massacre, the students of Leon take to the streets on July 23. They are machine-gunned by the National Guard: four students dead and more than 100 wounded.

vii

We left the country and organized, in San Jose, Costa Rica, the *Juventud Revolucionaria Nicaraguense* (Nicaraguan Revolutionary Youth). Carlos travelled to San Jose and to the Costa Rican banana zone — U.S. territory inhabited by Nicaraguans and a few Costa Ricans. He visited us in our refuge in San Jose, the neighborhoods where our brothers fixed shoes and dreams. With him, then and later, was Silvio Mayorga, hero and martyr of Pancasan.

Carlos went to Guatemala and Venezuela. He returned, underground for the first time, to Nicaragua. He attempted, though still a novice, to give the *Juventud Patriotica* (Patriotic Youth)* a new ideological content. He made a great impression on their leadership. The Socialist Party of course opposed such audacity, and published a note in the social column of its indefatigable newspaper announcing the arrival in Nicaragua of "that brave young student leader Carlos Fonseca." Immediately he was captured and expelled on an air force plane to Guatemala. From there he managed to get to Mexico

* Associated with the PSN.

where he met professor Edelberto Torres, for whom he always had a particular affection, one which we all later shared. Professor Torres wrote a book about Ruben Dario — known and appreciated among Hispanic intellectuals — which he dedicated to Carlos.†

From Mexico in 1961 he went to Honduras and became a member of the guerrilla column so brutally massacred at El Chaparral. The joint operation by the Honduran and Nicaraguan armies was a preview of CONDECA,* not yet born. The operation took its orders from the U.S. embassy in Tegucigalpa, Honduras. A shot from an M-1 carbine punctured Carlos's lung. As he didn't make a sound, the Honduran pigs thought him dead. Neither did he moan or cry on the painful ride to Tegucigalpa. They almost buried him. Silvio Mayorga and I were sitting in a cafe in San Jose when Doctor Enrique Lacayo Farfan, an honest man, brought us the news of Carlos's "death."

I began crying unashamedly (now I can tell you, Carlos) and I heard a Costa Rican say, "Look at that guy; he's crying for all he's worth." Silvio, who was also crying, said, "Don't be a fool." Carlos was badly wounded, but only wounded. Before the Chaparral events, Carlos had called us demanding we go to Tegucigalpa.

"But how," we asked, "if we don't have any money?" "I hope," he had responded, "that you have enough imagination to get there, even if you have to swim."

---

† "In my childhood, I read a lot of poetry, particularly that of Ruben Dario, the inevitable poet for any Nicaraguan." (Tomas Borge, in interview with Margaret Randall.)

* Central American Defense Council, established by the U.S. in 1964 to co-ordinate counter-insurgency activities in Central America.

Carlos Fonseca in Mexico
on the day of his wedding
to Maria Haydee Teran

Jose Benito Escobar
one of the first
militants of the FSLN

Silvio Mayorga Delgado
joint founder of the FSLN
with Tomas Borge and
Carlos Fonseca

viii

The next time we saw Carlos was in Cuba. In Havana he developed a close friendship with Tamara Bunke, fallen heroically in Bolivia. He also became friends with Commander Guevara.

Silvio went to Caracas and brought back a group of Nicaraguans to Cuba, where already there were other Nicaraguans joyfully walking the jubilant streets of Havana. Later these were the Sandinista guerrillas at Bocay y Rio Coco.

Carlos went to Honduras to prepare for our return. In July 1961, in the city of Tegucigalpa, in the presence of Carlos Fonseca, Silvio Mayorga, "Mister" Noel Guerrero,* and yours truly, the Sandinista National Liberation Front was born. The first militants of the FSLN were Santos Lopez, Jorge Navarro, Rigoberto Cruz, Francisco Buitrago, Faustino Ruiz, Jose Benito Escobar, Victor Tirado and German Pomares.

The name of the organization was suggested by, fought for, and finally won by Carlos.

* An ironic reference to a man who left the revolutionary movement after unsuccessful attempts to manipulate power within the FSLN. This is the "fourth" founder of the FSLN.

nineteen sixty

Guerrilla movement in the mountains of Nicaragua. Fallen in combat are Chale Haslam, farmer; Manuel Diaz Sotelo, journalist; Julio Alonso, ex-member of the National Guard; and Heriberto Reyes, veteran Sandinista.

Juventud Patriotica Nicaraguense (Patriotic Nicaraguan Youth) is organized inside the country and *Juventud Revolucionaria Nicaraguense* (Young Revolutionary Nicaraguans) outside the country.

ix

In 1962 the incipient revolutionary organization gathered 60 men on the shores of the Patuca River in Honduras. They trained there almost a year in the jungle, surrounded by birds, deer, roaring currents and ticks.

The first to explore the Patuca, where the guerrilla column was training, were Carlos Fonseca and Colonel Santos Lopez. And so, two generations of Nicaraguans came together, linked by the historic presence of Sandinista thought. Colonel Santos Lopez had been a member of the Choir of Angels, one of Sandino's combat units — adolescents specializing in commando actions. Those sweet and violent children — experts in winning difficult military objectives as well as the smiles of young women, who would join them in conspiratorial or romantic meetings.

The relationship between Carlos and Colonel Santos Lopez was not coincidental. The old and new generations of Sandinistas sought each other out in those dark times and found one another at the precise political moment. The old Sandinistas passed on their experiences, and we nurtured them in fields hungry for seeds and new perspectives. What was really taking place was the transference of all that which had been written about Sandino's struggle in the flesh, bones and words of the surviving veterans.

Almost immediately thereafter the first militants of the FSLN arrived at the Patuca: Victor Tirado and German Pomares (among those who survived);* Faustino Ruiz, Modesto Duarte, Francisco Buitrago, Rigoberto Cruz, Mauricio Cordoba and Silvio Mayorga (among the fallen). We had serious contradictions with "Mister" Guerrero and those kept Carlos from being able to participate in the guerrilla column. He was forced to return to Nicaragua secretly.

The Patuca guerrillas later made their way to the Bocay y Rio Coco, and engaged the National Guard in several combats. Those half-naked and undernourished men went one day without food; the next day it was hunger and dizziness; and a few days later it was *leismaniasis* (mountain leprosy), dizziness and hunger. The chief was chosen by weekly rotation. A leader like Carlos was needed.

The guerrillas made it back to Honduras with difficulty: naked, unarmed, on the verge of starvation, and — interestingly — when at last one of the group had consolidated himself as its leader.

In their contacts with the enemy a number of comrades fell. They continue to be reference points of generosity, heroism, joy and sacrifice among our present-day Sandinista militants. How can I forget — even in these brief notes — Jorge Navarro: our happy, optimistic and severe *Navarrito*, whose anecdotes made us laugh and who could milk our reserves of energy even at the most difficult times?

How can I fail to remember, even within the four walls of this cell, the gestures and words of Faustino Ruiz, *El*

---

* Victor Tirado Lopez is now one of the nine members of the FSLN's National Directorate. German Pomares was killed during the fall "offensive" of 1978 after this was written.

36

Jorge Navarro
the happy, optimistic and
severe *Navarrito* who
carried out the first
act of "economic recovery"

Rigoberto Cruz Perez—
known better as the legendary
Pablo Ubeda—who organized
peasants in the mountains
around Matagalpa

Santos Lopez. As a youth he
was a commando in
Sandino's Choir of Angels.
In 1961 he began training the
first combatants of the FSLN

Cuje, who never held out his hand unless it was to give you something, who never uttered a word that wasn't a sure arrow to the heart?

Francisco Buitrago and Modesto Duarte had a fight because Chico wanted Modesto to be the squadron chief and Modesto wanted it to be Chico. Colonel Santos Lopez had to decide, in front of Modesto's furrowed brow and Francisco's laughing eyes: his choice, of course, was Modesto.

There was also the comrade — whose name has unfortunately slipped my mind — who pretended he was eating so he could secretly give his rations to the weakest. Only those who have experienced guerrilla hunger know what that really means.

nineteen sixty-one

The Sandinista National Liberation Front is born. On the shores of the Patuca River, in Honduras, combatants unite under the leadership of Colonel Santos Lopez, veteran Sandinista.

Guerrilla squadrons are organized in the urban areas, under the leadership of Carlos Fonseca and Jorge Navarro. The first workers' and students' cells are founded in Managua and Leon, and the first groups of peasants come together in Chinandega, Matagalpa, Esteli, Somoto and Ocotal.

X

Inside the country, in Managua and Matagalpa, Carlos along with Jorge Navarro — he who had 33,000 cordobas in his pocket and walked so as not to spend organization money on a bus — organized the first Sandinista cells and the first armed group in the Matagalpa mountains.

Jorge Navarro, under Fonseca's leadership, planned and carried out the first act of "economic recovery" at a local bank: 35,000 cordobas, complete, sent to the mountains. Jorge read a message written by Carlos over Somoza's *Radio Mundial* — occupied with enthusiastic, awkward violence. Navarro later joined the guerrilla group at Bocay.

nineteen sixty-three

In March a guerrilla squadron led by Jorge Navarro occupies *Radio Mundial* and reads an FSLN proclamation in which we denounce the meeting taking place in San Jose, Costa Rica, between John Kennedy and the Central American presidents. Attending for Nicaragua are our recently imposed puppet president Rene Schick and the dynasty's clan member Luis Somoza.

In May we bring off another act of economic recovery when a Sandinista squadron occupies the Bank of America in Managua.

On June 23 the village of Raiti is occupied by an FSLN guerrilla unit. The commissary is expropriated and food and clothing are distributed among the population. The village of Gualaquistan is taken. There is fighting in Sang Sang, where Silvio Mayorga is wounded, and a National Guard officer and several soldiers are killed. In these actions we lose Jorge Navarro, Francisco Buitrago, Ivan Sanchez, Boanerges Santamaria, Modesto Duarte, and Faustino Ruiz. Pablo Ubeda, with the help of local people, is able to get to Las Bayas near Matagalpa where he begins far-reaching and fundamental work among the peasants.

xi

Carlos always said in his writings that the guerrilla experiences at Bocay y Rio Coco weren't *focos** and that the FSLN was born in defense of the exploited classes and was linked to them through the placenta. And it's true: the FSLN extended the warmth of its early hands to factories, neighborhoods, the university and the countryside around Matagalpa, Managua, Ocotal and Chinandega. When Victor Tirado and I returned to Nicaragua after the events of 1963, there were already three proletarian cells in Managua and a number of contacts with agricultural workers on the outskirts of the city. When we were on the shores of the Patuca, Silvio made it to Chinandega thanks to the political work carried out around El Viejo. It's true that the column headed into an unknown zone, inhabited by a sparse and marginalized population without political perspectives, but that was the guerrilla leadership's error rather than something traceable to the young revolutionary organization's orientations or class perspective.

* Literally, the "foco" theory, a misreading of the Cuban experience and of the theoretical work by French political writer Regis Debray, which nevertheless did show there was some possibility of guerrilla groups creating their own support networks in the mountains.

Proof of this, Carlos argued, was the fact that the FSLN survived the terrible setbacks of 1963 and 1967, as opposed to other guerrilla efforts in Latin America, most of which disappeared once they were defeated militarily leaving only the memories of their heroic footsteps. The FSLN, on the other hand, was able to strengthen itself, in political terms, after each of its military defeats. It is impossible to analyse the survival and development of the Sandinista organization unless we understand the clear architecture of its roots in the socially oppressed and exploited sectors of our society.

nineteen sixty-four

Work in the mountainside is broadened under the leadership of Rigoberto Cruz — the legendary Pablo Ubeda — with the participation of Carlos Reyna, Fausto Garcia and Carlos Tinoco. This organizing effort extends to the departments of Matagalpa, Jinotega and Zelaya. Unions and Sandinista cells are established in Uluse, El Bijao, La Tronca, Agua Maria, Cerro Colorado, Cuskaguas, Yaosca, El Carmen, Cubali, Guaslala, El Garrobo, El Kun, El Naranjo, El Ocote, Fila Grande, Pancasan and El Tuma. Literacy schools are set up in the mountains and peasants are sent to Managua where there is an attempt at providing them with revolutionary training.

xii

Carlos Fonseca's authority as leader of the FSLN was consolidated in 1963. The military blows received at Bocay y Rio Coco imposed a retreat which led us to place particular importance on work in the poor neighborhoods of Managua and other cities. This work was carried out in conjunction with the Socialist Party and with the defunct *Movilizacion Republicana* (Republican Mobilization).* Speeches and struggles around specific issues were the order of the day. Fortunately, the FSLN never abandoned the mountains nor the villages. On the first of every month Carlos met with Rigoberto Cruz (Pablo Ubeda) and other cadre, who were making significant gains organizing peasants in El Bijao, La Tronca and Uluse, mountainous regions in the department of Matagalpa. These were incipient union organizations but imbued with a political consciousness that laid the base for today's guerrilla movement.

Carlos said that the movement at Bocay y Rio Coco was the first action organized by a politically homogenous group. It was, he added, a kind of feeling-out of the

* Short-lived political alliance that the FSLN took part in.

revolutionary sector.

In some of his writings, Carlos maintained that the defeats suffered at Rio Coco pushed the FSLN toward reformist positions. It wasn't that we gave up on armed struggle, he explained in *La Hora Cero* (Zero Hour), but that we interrupted that kind of work for a time to continue the preparation. The factor that influenced this weakness, he added, was that the defeat of 1963 coincided with a general decline in the anti-Somoza struggle as a whole.

The FSLN leadership wasn't able to understand, at that time, that this decline was only a partial phenomena, and that the essential curve of the revolutionary movement was one of progress, on its way to maturity. In 1964-65 the FSLN in the cities aimed almost all its energies at above-ground work with the masses, particularly in the poorer neighborhoods of Managua and Leon.

On the other hand, intensive political work was being carried out structuring clandestine support networks in the rural and mountain areas.

Mainstay of this effort was our comrade Rigoberto Cruz (Pablo Ubeda) who, being a worker disguised as a medicine man, became a peasant down through his manner of speaking, to the way he walked Matagalpa's difficult geography and even to his habit of tossing pebbles in those night-time sessions where young country men and women go to light up the moon. From the point of view of his ideological and political concepts, Pablo Ubeda always remained a worker.

nineteen sixty-six

Renewal of armed struggle. We sabotage the Liberal Nationalist Party's convention, where Anastasio Somoza Debayle is proclaimed presidential candidate. Economic recoveries are carried out on a number of the country's banks. A group of Sandinistas under the leadership of Oscar Turcios participate in a kind of training course with the Guatemalan guerrilla movement headed by Luis Turcios Lima.

xiii

In 1965 Carlos was captured, along with Victor Tirado Lopez, in one of Managua's outlying neighborhoods. Condemned under the Quintana Law, he spent six months in prison, where he was visited by a sweet young woman who was later to become his wife. In prison he wrote the courageous document *Yo acuso* (I accuse). When his time was up, they exiled him once more — again aboard an express plane — to Guatemala. He was confined to El Peten, where he met and made friends with Lieutenant Luis Turcios Lima, future commander of Guatemala's Revolutionary Armed Forces (FAR). Turcios gave him several books on military tactics. Carlos escaped to Mexico, where he married Maria Haydee Teran. His wife and children are now safe in fraternal Cuba. He returned to Nicaragua in 1966.

nineteen sixty-seven

The FSLN concentrates on building a guerrilla base in the Dario mountains. The economic recoveries continue, and the Sandinista Front issues a communique denouncing the electoral farce.

On January 22 an anti-Somoza demonstration is machine-gunned. More than 400 people are killed.

In September the National Guard penetrates the Dario mountains. They repress the peasant population. Peasant leaders Eufresinio Davila, Eucadio Picado, Moises Picado, Felipe Gaitan and his five children are tortured and assassinated. Armando Flores, a young Sandinista combatant, is skinned alive with a razor blade, sprinkled with salt and left to die in unspeakable agony.

After prolonged resistance, Silvio Mayorga, Rigoberto Cruz, Francisco Moreno, Otto Casco, Fausto Garcia, the guerrilla doctor Danilo Rosales and Nicolas Sanchez (the "Tiger of Cerro Colorado") are killed in combat.*

In September accounts are settled with Gonzalo Lacayo, the most infamous torturer of those times, when

* Refers to the military defeat at Pancasan, an important reference point for the FSLN.

49

he is assassinated in Managua. In prison they murder the Sandinista Luciano Vilchez, known as the "Lion of El Dorado." On November 4, in broad daylight in Managua, they capture the important student leader and member of the FSLN's Directorate, Casimiro Sotelo, as well as Edmundo Perez, Hugo Medina and Roberto Amaya. Their bodies are finally handed over; there are obvious signs of torture.

xiv

The electoral process and its bloody outgrowth on January 22, 1967 defined our differences with other political groups. While the Socialist Party and the Republican Mobilization took part in the campaign with loudspeakers, signatures and fiery exhortations to unite with the bourgeois opposition — all of which, needless to say, fell on deaf ears — the FSLN moved its most valuable cadre into the mountains. Leading them as unquestioned political and military chief was Carlos Fonseca.

The Pancasan and Fila Grande guerrilla experiences sealed our political destiny once and for all. Sandino was no longer a name or one more date on the yearly calendar of activities, but truly a path.

In 1966 practical measures were taken — Carlos speaks of this in *Zero Hour* — to renew the armed actions. In that year the Sandinista Front became conscious of the deviations it had fallen into as a result of the blows suffered in 1963, and proceeded with preparation of the guerrilla base at Pancasan. Although this preparation was an improvement with respect to organizational work over the FSLN's armed initiatives in 1963, in terms of political and military tactics it did not represent a serious advance. It was an organizational improvement because it was no longer the preparation of an armed movement from a neighboring country — distant from the main enemy — but instead was the preparation of an armed movement from the mountains in the middle of our own homeland.

nineteen sixty-eight

In April David and Rene Tejada, ex-officers of the National Guard and FSLN members, are captured and beaten by Somoza's personal aide, Major Oscar Morales. David dies as a result of the blows and his body is thrown into the smoldering crater of the Santiago Volcano, provoking protest around the world.

XV

At 6 in the afternoon the news came. Carlos was lost after an encounter with a local strongman. The guide who was with him couldn't find him in the dark. The violent exchange of gunfire led one to imagine that Carlos was either wounded or dead. No one knew, because he was one of those wounded who never let on he was alive. The mere possibility of his death crushed us. It couldn't be. Not now. Not ever. We were too tender, and besides: what about the friend, the brother, the exemplary leader?

In the encounter a horse was killed and the strongman wounded. Carlos managed to make it to the home of a peasant collaborator. Fifteen days later he showed up at the camp, bearded, gaunt, bawling everyone out.

xvi

The military defeat at Pancasan, which naturally meant a new period of retreat, showed the FSLN to be a historic answer, the necessary synthesis of more than a hundred years of people's struggle. The organization gained in political authority, especially if one considers the fact that Pancasan coincided with the ebbtide in armed struggle throughout Latin America. Only a few days after our battle, Commander Enesto Guevara died heroically in Bolivia. Javier Heraud, the adolescent poet who left a mark on his country's literature — another Leonel Rugama — fell in the mountains of Peru "among birds and trees," fulfilling the promise of one of his beautiful poems. Hugo Blanco and Hector Bejar, Peruvian guerrilla leaders, were captured by that country's army, thereby liquidating what had seemed a promising armed effort. Turcios Lima was dead in Guatemala.

Those were hard times, times when difficulties were the bread of each and every circumstance. The dogmatic and the weak discovered, once more, the ironic smiles they had misplaced years before. Carlos neither lost sight of reality nor did he abandon his harmonious, historic stubbornness. He continued to work patiently, linking scattered efforts, facing local dangers and contradictions. And he sharpened his critical sense.

On the other hand, Pancasan meant the last of the remnants of *foquismo*. In the guerrilla zone itself, work was carried out that took other forces into consideration. For instance, political work continued in the regions around Managua and other cities. Attention was paid to student and union organizing, and contacts were established with leaders of the traditional political parties, intellectuals and priests.

After Pancasan, an accumulation of forces is initiated in silence, and begins — slowly — sculpting a growing organic structure in working-class neighborhoods and rural areas.

nineteen sixty-nine

Political work is strengthened in the Matagalpa mountains and in the cities of Managua, Leon and Esteli. There is a proliferation of intensive courses in political and military preparation.

In the northern mountains, particularly in Yaosca, National Guard patrols headed by noncommissioned officer Miguel Tinoco repress the peasant population. Murder, rape, torture and the burning of shacks multiply. In Costa Rica, through joint operations by that country's and Nicaragua's security forces, several Sandinista leaders are captured: among them Carlos Fonseca, Oscar Turcios, Humberto Ortega, Henry Ruiz and Tomas Borge.

On July 15, the home of national FSLN leader Julio Buitrago is discovered and attacked by more than 400 national guardsmen, complete with artillery and air support. For more than three hours Julio fights to his death. It is a battle of one man against an army. As a result, we began to say that there might be men in this world as heroic as Julio Buitrago, but none more heroic. The same day, in a similar operation, we lose Antonio Rivera, Anibal Castrillo and Alesio Blandon. These events won admiration and a profound respect for the FSLN. Numerous young people ask to be admitted to the organization.

xvii

They had discovered all the houses. Lesbia was taken prisoner; she knew the last of the hiding places. With Velia we went out looking for any old place where we could stay, and found an abandoned house where the rats were like cats and holes like windows. Carlos stretched out his long legs on the floor; we gave Velia the only blanket. A week later we had five safehouses in that neighborhood.

Carlos Aguero Echeverria
who freed Carlos
Fonseca from a Costa Rican
prison in 1969

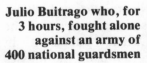

Julio Buitrago who, for
3 hours, fought alone
against an army of
400 national guardsmen

xviii

In 1969 the leadership of the FSLN reorganized. Carlos was named General Secretary. The Program and Statutes were published. Carlos wrote *Zero Hour*. He went again to Costa Rica, intent on developing a new guerrilla project, one that later showed its face at Bijao and Zinica. But he was suddenly captured by the Costa Rican police. We retrieved him in the famous attack on the Alajuela prison, but he was recaptured. Carlos Aguero directed the action that finally succeeded in obtaining Fonseca's freedom. From prison Carlos went to Cuba, where he stayed several years, never distancing himself from Nicaragua nor from the FSLN.

In Cuba he wrote *Viva Sandino* (Long Live Sandino), a book which has yet to circulate in Nicaragua* and which, without doubt, represents the first serious analysis of the history of Sandinism. In an article published in *Tricontinental* magazine, he urged organizing the masses throughout the entire country.

* It is, of course, widely available now, and was recently published in English by the Department of Propaganda and Political Education of the FSLN, Managua.

And that's just what we did. The FSLN donned long pants to walk the mountains, villages, counties, slums, factories, universities, high schools. We grew, perhaps, too fast.

xix

During those endless conversations in which we consumed quantities of coffee, cigarettes and dawns, Carlos would say, referring to the role of the working class, the peasants and the petit-bourgeoisie:

"From the time the FSLN gained momentum — and even before — we've always said that the working class is destined by history to lead the victorious revolution. And even more important, in spite of the limitations of our country's economic development, our organization always sought out the factories and other production centers. But to under-estimate the role of the peasants, in this nation of battered, hungry and dispossessed country people, with their own tradition of struggle, would be, in practice, a renunciation of revolutionary struggle. It would be the easy road to legality, surrendering to our enemy and sleeping on the blood of our martyrs."

Of course the working class is not a metaphor. Neither is it an abstraction. It exists in a tangible geography, and one can come to it along a path weighed down by the unsatisfied demands of the poor. Reality often demands that political cadre go the rural route in their journey to a center of production. The FSLN's National Directorate demanded of its intermediate cadre that they pay special attention to factories and also to workers outside of the factories, in the neighborhoods.

The armed detachment in the mountains — vanguard of, and guarantee for, our revolutionary process — had a significant percentage of workers in its ranks, aside from the fact that being in the mountains in itself means proletarianization. Once, when we checked the class origin of our militancy in a given region, almost all were workers from one or another production center. Workers who had distinguished themselves by their determination and ability were given positions of leadership among the masses, were made leaders of guerrilla columns or given the responsibility for a region or a zone.

The working class, Carlos Fonseca said, doesn't spontaneously assume its vanguard position. The rapidity with which the working class recognizes its historic role depends on a variety of factors: industrial development, the political level of the masses, and the capacity of the revolutionaries.

In the last analysis, the organized revolutionary movement provides the energy capable of unleashing the conscious participation of the working class.

nineteen seventy

A considerable number of Sandinistas, mainly peasants, gather in the mountainous area of El Bijao, department of Matagalpa.

On January 2, a Sandinista squadron led by the poet Leonel Rugama and including — among others — Roger Nunez and Mauricio Hernandez, carries out an economic recovery against the bank at El Arbolito in Managua.

On January 15, Leonel — the best poet of his generation — Roger and Mauricio were discovered in their safehouse. More than 300 soldiers of the National Guard appear on the scene with helicopters and tanks. The three Sandinistas, with their simple arms, fight with heroism. The sound of machine-gun fire and the blasts from the tanks are unable to still their war songs or combat cries, until they die riddled with bullets in those smoking ruins. In mass demonstrations, thousands of people show their support for the three guerrillas with a unanimous cry of "Homeland or Death."

In February, on one more anniversary of the murder of our national hero Augusto Cesar Sandino, Sandinista squadrons place explosives in the homes of some of Somoza's military and political henchmen. On February

21 a guerrilla squadron reads an FSLN communique over *Radio Mundial.*

That same month the Pablo Ubeda column, camped near the Waslala River, is detected. Two hundred National Guardsmen penetrate the mountains, leading three patrols from different directions to where the guerrilla camp is located. On February 11 a patrol made up of 40 men, approaching from Las Vallas, is held at bay by a Sandinista lookout. The enemy suffers one wounded there.

The camp was evacuated by the guerrillas. Most regroup at El Bijao where our leader Oscar Turcios joins them.

The enemy unleashes an intensive campaign of vigilance and repression against the peasant population. Local agents assassinate the Sandinista combatants Luis Cabo Hernandez and Jesus Mendez, both peasants.

A National Guard patrol in Wamblan murders nineteen members of a family by the name of Moncada. In Kilambe they kill Alfonso Torrez and two workers, and rape two peasant sisters by the name of Martinez. At La Gloria near the El Carmen ranch, a National Guard patrol captures several young peasants whose whereabouts were reported by the rich landowner Marcelino Castro. Tortured to death are 34-year-old Julio, 25-year-old Toribio, 18-year-old Doroteo, 14-year-old Julian, and 9-year-old Daniel, all members of the Ramos family.

Juan Saturnino Gonzalez and Juan Hernandez Lopez are captured at Cua. They disappear in a military helicopter. At Las Vallas, Juan and Gabino Hernandez Sanchez are murdered.

Several old women, among them Venancia Hernandez, who is 98, are captured and tortured at Cua. The young peasant women Candida Donaire Romero and Angela Garcia are raped. The chief of the repressive forces is the National Guard Captain Manuel Sandino, Lieutenant Juan Lee Wong is his second in command.

April 3, in Leon, several Sandinista combatants intercept the National Guard investigations chief and kill him. The enemy unleashes a repressive operation throughout the city, discovering the Sandinistas Luisa Amanda Espinosa and Enrique Lorente, who hold off several enemy patrols with helicopter support until they fall in combat.

In May, the Sandinista combatant Igor Ubeda dies after wounding a National Guard mercenary on guard at a bank the guerrillas tried to attack.

In July, in Jinotega, the young peasant Sandinista Efren Ortega is murdered while carrying out his duties as messenger.

In August, Sandinistas Edwin Melendez, Orlando Castrillo and Noel Arguello are machine-gunned when they try to make contact with the guerrillas in the mountains.

Several repressive agents are brought to justice in Esteli. Local strongmen in the habit of ratting on unionized peasants are also brought to justice, mainly in the departments of Matagalpa and Jinotega.

On September 5, in an FSLN act of solidarity with the just cause of the Arab peoples, the Sandinista combatant Patricio Arguello is mortally wounded when he tries, along with Palestinian guerrillas, to hijack a Zionist plane in French skies. In a later hijacking, also over Europe, in which Juan Jose Quezada participates, we manage to retrieve Arguello's body and to obtain the freedom of a Palestinian woman guerrilla.

XX

The eleven-year-old girl was swollen and dying, her big eyes mature as those of an adult. She told us she didn't want to die. She was starving. Carlos looked at her, his forehead deeply furrowed. I took the girl in my arms while my brother paced in desperation. She flickered out like a lamp burning its last drop of kerosene. I couldn't wipe my eyes because my arms were busy rocking her. Carlos flung himself into his hammock and began to smoke.

xxi

"Unfortunately, in Nicaragua" — Carlos would say, referring to an old headache — "the petit-bourgeosie is reactionary, politically ignorant and ill-inclined. In this country, those with a petit-bourgeois formation break easily, can't put up with the rigors of the guerrilla campaigns, are incapable of keeping their dignity and positions of solidarity when hard times hit, but are the first to pee euphorically when times are good."

That's the way it was. After the December 27 action,* they were the most enthusiastic revolutionaries in the world. On the other hand, with the setbacks at El Sauce and Ocotal, their ardor turned to objections, their fearful eyes to the past.

---

* The hostage-taking incident at the Chema Castillo residence, where the FSLN was able to negotiate the release of political prisoners, a $2 million ransom and the publishing and broadcasting of FSLN communiques.

nineteen seventy-one

On October 21, a commando hijacks a plane in Costa Rica and takes four yankee United Fruit officials hostage, obtaining freedom for our leader Carlos Fonseca Amador and our comrades Humberto Ortega, Plutarco Hernandez and Rufo Marin. The Sandinista Fabian Rodriguez is assassinated near Matagalpa.

xxii

Carlos ordered us to switch camps. We came to the edge of a precipice and installed ourselves on a tiny rise. During the night Silvio, Carlos and Chelito Moreno burned with fever, vomited and had diarrhea. In the morning we gave them chloranfenicol. Three days later Socrates the doctor arrived, and told us the diagnosis was correct. Our brothers had paratyphoid.

xxiii

"Implacable in combat; generous in victory." That was what we said in a public document about that time. The phrase synthesized our concept of our contradictions with the enemy. A phrase as old as the FSLN, identical to Carlos Fonseca's way of being, to his unlimited generosity.

He used to tell us: "Victory has a high and sorrowful price. Complete joy, for that very reason, belongs to the future generations; it's for them that we are fighting this war. Nonetheless, we must avoid unnecessary sacrifice, minimize tears and bloodshed. The National Guard soldiers, as individuals, are part of our people. Blind instruments, unfortunately, of the soul-less oligarchs and their foreign masters. If we take a national guardsman prisoner, not only must we respect his life and dignity, we must treat him like one of our own brothers. Better to sin on the side of generosity even if it's not rigorously just. The important thing — as Fidel once said — is to do away with sin and save the sinner."

Some of those who doubtless took pleasure in his death, owe their own lives to our leader, who always counselled against radical measures when it came to punishment; punishment which might so easily have been inspired by the indignation and revolt the enemy's crimes and abuses produced in us.

"If we allow ourselves to be guided by our personal sentiments" — he would say — "by our anger, by the understandable impulse of 'an eye for an eye, a tooth for a tooth,' we will be guilty of the very sins we are fighting against. If we wish to build a society inhabited by a new kind of human being, must we not act like new human beings? If we mistreat or kill our prisoners, how are we different from our enemies?"

xxiv

The young peasant didn't want us to shoot him. He had deserted, taking with him his revolver and 50 cordobas. We came to his parents' hut. His mother said, "Forgive him, please, it was a fit of craziness." Carlos said, let him go. The young peasant joined the guerrillas at Zinica.

XXV

Among his last words, written in the mountains, is a call to revise our work methods:

"Certain contrasts can best express particular ideas. For example, there are tasks in the rural areas that are impossible for a student to assume, in spite of the fact that there are proletarianized students who must carry out certain indispensable jobs in that area. At the same time, there are tasks within the university context that militants with an exclusively peasant background cannot undertake. This, aside from the fact that it is important for the revolutionary, wherever he or she may be, to relate in some way to the lives of working people."

Carlos contributed notably to the formation of the Sandinista militant. He preached with example and with his word, his fraternity, his discipline, the pleasure he took in sacrifice, and his total lack of egotism. It is amazing and moving how young extroverts from a country that specializes in exporting beautiful and precise words, surrounded by corruption and selfishness, can be serious, respectful, discreet, modest and impeccable. They fight like lions in uneven combat, they sing and laugh when they are dropping from fatigue, and they blush at the recognition and admiration of all the peoples of the world. Throughout its entire history, the FSLN learned how to place each of its militants in his or her precise place.

Correct leadership, Carlos always said, discovers the positive and fruitful aspects in each member of the organization, in order to channel them in favor of the movement as a whole; while at the same time pointing out each member's negative aspects in order to limit the effects these might have on the life of the organization.

He emphasized the fact that we must never cover up for the organization's weaknesses, but at the same time we should close our ears to the insolence of those who would only see a negative balance in the road travelled so far.

xxvi

German Pomares (*El Danto*) and I were training a group of peasants, several young men and a young woman. We taught them how to arm and disarm the Garand, the M-1 carbine, the M-3 sub-machinegun and the 45 pistol. When Carlos arrived, he told us, "Teach them to read as well."

xxvii

Referring to the unity of the revolutionary movement, Carlos said:

"We learn from the great experiences of other peoples, that the unity of a revolutionary movement has its source in the fundamental similarity of interests that motivate the deepest dreams of thousands and thousands of workers and dispossessed within a given society.

"It's not negative, it is in fact positive, that a wide variety of opinions about the possible solutions to these problems emerge. This is nothing new, and it has been a part of other victorious struggles, as well as of all historic processes dating from ancient times. In the *Iliad* itself we read about the differences that surfaced among a single band of fighters. It's also worth noting that this story tells of the role older combatants can play to bring about harmony in this respect.

"Something that isn't really known about the Cuban revolution are the heated discussions that took place as late as July 1958 concerning the role of armed actions in the mountains."

Eduardo Contreras
who led the commando which
occupied the house of
a high-ranking member of
the Somoza regime

**German Pomares
Ordonez (*El Danto*)
who taught peasants
how to read
and how to shoot**

nineteen seventy-four

The Juan Jose Quezada commando occupies the home of Doctor Jose Maria Castillo, a high-ranking member of the Somoza regime. A party in honor of the yankee ambassador was taking place at the house.

While high government officials and members of the diplomatic corps are taken hostage, the commando — led by Eduardo Contreras — demands the release of the Sandinista prisoners, 5 million U.S. dollars, a minimum pay raise for National Guard recruits and the publication in newspapers and over the radio of the two FSLN communiques.

The regime gives in to the most important demands.

The action receives international attention, and initiates a new stage of struggle.

Guerrilla warfare in the mountains is intensified under the leadership of Henry Ruiz and Carlos Aguero.

The repression broadens and deepens, martial law is instituted and a permanent military court is in session.

xxviii

Speaking of the language to be used among comrades, Carlos recommended:

"We must do everything possible to use a persuasive and fraternal tone, while being careful to remain true to our objectives, avoid calling people names as this only tends to aggravate the problem instead of solving it."

And he added:

"In spite of the weaknesses and mistakes we carry with us, we must say that the balance of twenty years (since we renewed our decision to take up arms September 21, 1956) is positive. The balance of work carried out by the Sandinista Front over all these years is a positive one. It is impossible to simplify an entire process such as this one, but in an attempt at clarity and brevity, we'll answer the following question: what is it that more than anything else shows us the positive balance achieved? The steel in the underground urban militant and in the militant of the rural guerrilla. Great revolutionaries have said that a revolution may be judged by its capacity to grow. And in Nicaragua, from the time we recruited the first peasant hut and the first urban safehouse in 1961, it has been possible to raise a whole column of combatants made of steel, feared by the gangsters who rule Nicaragua and the only hope for a people so long submerged in pain.

"Yet, is it enough to have forged these militants made of steel? No. We must respond as fully as possible to the question of what is possible to do and by what means will we be able to do it, based on the organization we have at hand. If we can't answer this question, we run the risk of the steel eroding."

xxix

He couldn't walk. He had sores on his feet and his right big toe nail had become inflamed. We got to the camp and Rigoberto examined his feet. The toe was infected and we had no anaesthesia. Carlos stuck a handkerchief in his mouth; we immobilized the foot and Rigoberto took a knife and extracted pus, the nail and a few cries. Carlos sweated and so did we. Who said anything about resting? The march continued at 4 the following morning, slowly, with our leader limping and impossible. The Chinaman said, in his sweet voice, "What a brute we have for a commander."

XXX

It is impossible to refer explicitly to Carlos Fonseca's thought, much less quote from his writings — in magazines, pamphlets, and books containing the political views of our General Secretary — because for obvious reasons I do not have them at hand. And so I would like to make clear, for the sake of literary honesty, that the words in this text attributed to Carlos are not, in most cases, exact quotes. I've tried to reflect the content — and whenever possible the form — of his thought. Fonseca expressed these and other ideas at different moments in his exemplary life much more correctly and clearly than I can.

xxxi

With our fallen brother's example before us, the Sandinista revolution marches today toward a vigorous renewal. We measure our dreams against history's answers. Sandinista optimism is objective, naked as a young horse. The revolution that gave birth to Fonseca is a mother who carries in her womb new and definitive answers: the victory of Sandino, the victory of the blood of Carlos, the victory always, heroes and martyrs.

As I only recently said when making a declaration before the military courts: Today, for us, for our people, dawn is no longer beyond our reach. Tomorrow, one day, soon, an as-yet-unknown sun will shine on that earth our heroes and martyrs promised us. An earth with rushing rivers of milk and honey, where human beings will be as brothers and sisters, where love, generosity and heroism will be everyday events. At the doors of our world a guardian angel will wield a fiery sword against the return of selfishness, arrogance, disdain, corruption, violence and the cruel and aggressive exploitation of a few over many.

That's what we are fighting for, that's why Augusto Cesar Sandino, Carlos Fonseca and hundreds of Nicaraguan patriots and revolutionaries gave their lives.

xxxii

Our brother fell in a chance encounter. Little by little we've been able to gather information about the circumstances of his death. He was making his way to Modesto's camp with a group of comrades. Just beyond dusk, in the rain and along one of those pathways where calm is always suspect, they heard three revolver shots. The group took cover in the bush. Claudia, Carlos Aguero's lovely comrade, was able to observe — in sharp black and white — the light-footed step of a peasant man. They could all hear the shouts: the guy was drunk on *cususa*, ubiquitous alcoholic beverage made by the people of the mountains. Most probably he was a local strongman, and the author of the shots.

Carlos decided to wait 24 hours, and they resumed their march the following sundown. At the head of the group, the guide. Then Carlos. And bringing up the rear of seven men, Claudia. The first shot of a Garand* was heard and there was an immediate flush of birds. Seconds before the darkness was broken by machinegun fire, Carlos threw himself to the ground and shot his M-1 carbine, ordering the rest of the squadron to retreat. The combatants

---

* Rifle used by Somoza forces; it has a distinctive report.

Jamie Wheelock (left) and Tomas Borge— Comandantes of the Revolution and National Directorate members— beneath a poster of Carlos Fonseca

The burial of Carlos Fonseca

managed to crawl and take cover a short distance away. The explosion of numerous grenades and then total silence translated the painful fact: our chief and founder was dead.

The guerrillas remained where they were, observing the scene from the bush. In the morning there was an unusual number of helicopters. Laughter and shouts could be heard. High level officers arrived. They cut Carlos's head off and took it to the tyrant, who couldn't believe that this man persecuted by legend and hate was dead.*

Carlos died with his gun in hand, his heart overflowing with love, his blue eyes looking toward the future.

When the representatives of this selfish and brutal system are sad and all-but-forgotten historical references, when no one remembers the quacks and deserters, when the pale and powdered pawns of today are reduced to ashes, the free, joyful and generous generations of tomorrow will remember Carlos Fonseca.

The commander at the Tipitapa prison came to my small cell, jubilant, with a copy of *Novedades* in his hands. He gave me the news: "Carlos Fonseca is dead," he said. After a few moments of silence, I answered: "You're wrong, colonel. Carlos Fonseca is one of the dead who never die." The colonel said, "You guys are something else."

---

* Carlos Fonseca's body was buried and the grave cared for by a local peasant. In 1979, after the Sandinista victory, it was dug up and taken to Managua for burial in Revolution Square. The body was intact. The story that Tomas Borge tells was a rumor circulating at the time; in prison Borge had no access to more accurate information.

chronology

1936 Born on June 23 in El Laborio neighborhood of Matagalpa, Nicaragua, to the peasant woman Justina Fonseca, cook by trade, and to Fausto F. Amador, worker at an American-owned mine.

1942 Begins grade school at a boy's school in Matagalpa.

1945 To help his mother he peddles the candy she makes. From the age of 9 until he turns 14 he sells newspapers in the streets of Matagalpa. "Carlos was extremely studious, for him the toys and games of his peers did not exist; only books." (Berta Prado, "Carlos, un gran lector," *Barricada*, 9/11/80.)*

1950 After finishing grade school he works as a telegram messenger for two months, then enters secondary school at the National Institute in North Matagalpa.

1951 Works for two months, April and May, this time in the mineral water works *La Reina*. Also during this time Carlos sells grape leaves to Arab families in Matagalpa.

1952 Still trying to help his mother, he organizes a raffle of a Sacred Heart of Jesus statue with his friend Ramon Castillo. He gets the highest marks in his class in his third year of secondary school. With another friend, Tomas Borge, he also discovers fascinating reading material: Tomas Moro, John Steinbeck, Howard Fast.

* Taken from *Carlos Fonseca, Works: Volume I, Under the Sandinist Banner*, Managua: Editorial Nueva Nicaragua, 1981, pp. 431-440.

He participates in a strike at the Institute demanding the removal of a medallion depicting Somoza Garcia from the University of Leon crest.

1953 Fonseca and Borge discover Marx and Engels in the bookstore of the poet Samuel Meza. They read and study with a third friend, Ramon Gutierrez Castro, just arrived from Guatemala. Fonseca becomes sympathetic to UNAP (National Union for Popular Action) which tries to recruit independent youths into political parties but is soon dominated by conservatives. The left separates from UNAP and founds the Party for National Renewal. "I had a lot of enthusiasm for politics and I wanted better for Nicaragua, so I joined UNAP, and I went so far as becoming close with its leadership. I lost my enthusiasm when I realized they were all pampered boys who never showed any signs of having suffered the misery the people have suffered. I was very disillusioned." (Carlos Fonseca, "Declaration of September 27, 1956," after the assassination of the dictator Anastasio Somoza Garcia.)

1954 He and others found the magazine *Segovia*, and he produces the first four issues of the six that were put out. He publishes articles and poems, including "The Sixteen Verses of the *Molendero*."

He meets Marco A. Altamirano, who accompanies him to the seminars held by Ramon Gutierrez Castro. There they read the Communist Party manifesto, articles on the industrial revolution, workers' papers, etc. On their own, they read *Mother* by Gorki, and they sell *Unidad*, the Nicaraguan Socialist Party newspaper. "The sale took two days, since they would cover all the neighborhoods in Matagalpa, enter people's houses and read the potential customer the article in the paper." (Jesus Miguel Blandon, *Entre Sandino y Fonseca*, 1979, p. 85.)

1955 On March 4, he graduates from secondary school with the gold medal which is awarded to the best graduate each year. He goes to Managua and in May becomes director of the library at the Ramirez Goyena Institute, making 200 cordobas plus board. In June he enrolls in the School of Economics at the National University, but soon had to give up his studies because of student strikes. In July he joins the Socialist Party.

1956 He moves to Leon and works for *La Prensa*, making 200 cordobas without board. He enrolls in the Faculty of Law. He starts, with Silvio Mayorga, Tomas Borge and the Guatemalan Heriberto Carillo, the first group to agitate for working-class demands in a political context.

89

On September 27, six days after the killing of Anastasio Somoza Garcia by Rigoberto Lopez Perez, he is arrested in Matagalpa. Two issues of *El Universitario* are published by him and others on the presses of Edwin Castro, a friend of Rigoberto, who is imprisoned and later killed by government forces. In the meantime, the National Guard raids Fonseca's locker in Leon and confiscates a picture of his maternal brothers and "innocent things such as verse books by Cesar Vallejo and Emilio Quintana. Novels by William Faulkner. Books on politics written by Catholics like Cardenal Jose Maria Caro." (Carlos Fonseca, letter of December 11, 1957.) He is freed 50 days later. He remains in Matagalpa from December 12 to 31, studying to catch up on his neglected courses.

1957 He passes his first year at law school, scoring high marks in all his courses.

On July 3 he goes to Costa Rica and stays with Manolo Cuadra, who arranges a trip to Moscow for him. On July 24 he leaves for that city, travelling first through Havana, Miami, New York, Shannon (Ireland), Amsterdam, Zurich, Vienna (where he takes part in the fifth World Youth and Student Festival), Kiev (where he attends the Kiev Congress), Leipzig in East Germany (for the Congress of Students for Peace and Friendship), East Berlin, Leningrad and Prague. Returning home, he visits Mexico and San Jose, Costa Rica. On December 16, he arrives in Nicaragua and is detained at the airport. His luggage is returned but three books are seized, among them *Report from the Foot of the Gallows* by Julius Fucik, a Czech journalist. Also taken are his camera and a pen and pencil set. He moves into a boarding house on the south side of Los Bomberos park in Managua. His acquaintances there include Adan Selva, Aquiles Centeno, Rolando Steiner, Maria Theresa Sanchez, Manuel Diaz y Sotelo and Marco A Altamirano. "According to Marco, one of the books that helped form Carlos' humanitarian position was *Report from the Foot of the Gallows*...Fucik is about to turn in his comrades because they have threatened to kill his mother and sons. Then he hears the moan of a prisoner dragging his chains, and he decides to remain silent." (Blandon, p. 85.)

1958 In January he begins writing *Un Nicaraguense en Moscu* (A Nicaraguan in Moscow). In March he signs the Minimum Program of the Republican Mobilization Party which asks for general amnesty and the return of exiles. He circulates *Un Nicaraguense en Moscu*, prefaced by Manuel Perez Estrada and published by *Unidad*, the Socialist Party newspaper.

Returning to Leon in June, he is selected to give the opening speech for the 1958 curriculum year. In his capacity as a director for CUUN (University Centre for the National University) he organizes student assemblies to demand the freedom of various university professors and a student (Tomas Borge) imprisoned since the killing of Somoza Garcia. When he asks for financial support from the National Assembly of Students, he is taken prisoner in Managua, along with Rene Guandique Oviedo, on November 29. Soon he is freed, but in December he is again imprisoned in Matagalpa.

1959 He does not write his second year law exams in February. In March, with others, he organizes Democratic Nicaraguan Youth (JDN) which in the words of Carlos Fonseca and Silvio Mayorga "is the first attempt by Nicaraguan youth to become politically independent and play a historical role." The JDN paints slogans against the dictatorship, leads demonstrations and criticizes the National Opposition Union (UNO), run by the Conservative Party. In the repression that is unleashed, he is captured on April 2 with Silvio Mayorga and Fernando Ampie. On April 7 university organizations — CUUN, Law Students Association, and the JDN, Leon division — demand his release. On April 8 he is deported to Guatemala in an air force plane. In the Guatemalan capital he finds work with the Students' Association. He goes to Honduras to join the guerrilla column "Rigoberto Lopez Perez," in which the majority come from Cuba and which is led by an ex-National Guardsman. The column is massacred by Honduran and Nicaraguan troops in El Chaparral, Honduras, in June. In response, Leon students demonstrate and government forces fire machine-guns into the crowd, killing or wounding 100. Carlos, shot through the lung at El Chaparral, is transferred to a hospital in Tegucigalpa, Honduras, and there he is visited by his mother in August. He leaves in September for the Calixto Garcia hospital in Havana to finish his convalescence.

1960 On January 15 he arrives in Costa Rica and writes: "My desire to struggle for a new, better life for my compatriots has consolidated." He receives another brief visit from his mother. He travels to Venezuela to attend a convention of the Nicaraguan Unitarian Front (FUN) and on February 20 he signs, as a delegate from CUUN, the Minimum Program for that progressive organization. In March he develops, with Silvio Mayorga, a presentation, "Brief analysis of the popular struggle in Nicaragua against the Somoza dictatorship," for the Federation of the Central University of Venezuela University

Centres. Detained in Maiquetia airport, he is sent in May to Mexico, where he meets professor Edelberto Torres.

In June he returns to Nicaragua but he is captured and kept in the caves of La Curva for several weeks. In the middle of the night, he is removed from his cell and put on a plane that takes him to Guatemala. In July Guatemalan authorities confine him to El Peten, in the Upman region. Here he befriends Luis Augusto Turcios Lima, future *comandante* of the Revolutionary Armed Forces of Guatemala (FAR). Transferred to the capital, he is put under house arrest.

On November 29 he leaves for Havana without documentation. There waiting for him are Tomas Borge and Julio Jerez, who accompany him to Costa Rica and transfer him to Nicaragua. He makes contact with the recently founded Patriotic Nicaraguan Youth (JPN) which has carried out intense protest activities.

1961 He founds the New Nicaraguan Movement (MNN). Other founders include Enrique Lorente, Faustino Ruiz, Fernando Gordillo, Francisco Buitrago, German Pomares, Ivan Sanchez, Santos Lopez, Silvio Mayorga, Jorge Navarro, Jose Benito Escobar, Carlos Reyna, Tomas Borge, Rigoberto Lopez Cruz, Oscar Benavides, Eden Pastora, Julio Jerez, German Gaitan and Bayardo Altamirano. The MNN organizes three cells in Managua, Leon and Esteli. It denounces the preparations for the invasion of the Bay of Pigs, and in February it publishes the first Sandino ideology, selected by Carlos.

He travels again to Honduras where he meets with Tomas Borge, Silvio Mayorga, Faustino Ruiz and Santos Lopez. At this meeting in July, Carlos Fonseca proposes the name Sandinista National Liberation Front (FSLN) for the emerging armed revolutionary organization that has been developing for the last few months. In November he is in Nicaragua again, reunited with other comrades from the MNN, German Gaitan, Julio Jerez and others, in the house of Constantino Baltodano Zeledon. He returns to Honduras in December.

1962 On January 22 he enters Nicaragua. He returns to Honduras and then goes to Cuba. In May he travels to Caracas, Venezuela. He returns to Nicaragua to activate the Revolutionary Students Front (FER), then leaves again for Honduras. With the Sandinista veteran Santos Lopez, in July he enters the Olancho department and navigates the Patuca and Guayaca rivers to confirm the possibilities for armed struggle. He reaches the Coco river border with dozens of comrades, but his disagreements with Noel Guerrero Santiago (who shortly thereafter leaves the FSLN), and the need to strengthen the internal Front, prevent him from participating in the rural guerrilla activities and in December he travels to Matagalpa.

1963 He leaves again for Honduras in January and in February returns to Nicaragua. Against his will, due to his continued differences with and criticisms of the work methods of Noel Guerrero, he is forced to remain outside the combative zone. Instead he does organizing work, directing the formation of the internal *Frente*, the training schools, the armed operations that period — February to August — were carried out by the urban resistance. Between November and December he studies the Nicaraguan guerrilla movement and the revolutionary struggles of other peoples.

1964 After entering the country to strengthen the internal Front structures, in May he goes to Managua. On June 20 he is captured with Victor Tirado Lopez in the neighborhood of San Luis. On July 8 he writes the pamphlet, "I accuse the Dictatorship from my Cell." The next day he is sentenced to six months in prison. On September 21 he writes, "This is the Truth," an essay that refutes a government communique. In jail he is visited by Maria Haydee Teran, whom he later marries. It is their first meeting.

1965 On January 6 he is deported to Guatemala in a plane. "In this way," he wrote, "I have been expelled for the third time from Nicaragua, my cherished country. Yes, three times expelled in my young life from my Nicaragua. But the oppressors of my country should keep one thing very clear. And that is, they can expel my body from Nicaragua, but they will never expel from my spirit the desire to fight for Nicaragua's freedom and sovereignty and her people's happiness." He is confined again in *El Peten*, but on the night of January 15 he is freed in a guerrilla raid on the prison. The next day he arrives in Tapachula, Mexico and meets Rodolfo Tapia Molina.

He maintains contact with the FSLN. On March 20, still in Mexico, he is married to Maria Haydee Teran through a power of attorney in a civil ceremony in Leon. The religious ceremony takes place in Mexico, at the house of Edelberto Torres, who is best man.

In mid-year he moves to San Jose, Costa Rica. From September to December he does research on Ruben Dario for his teacher Edelberto Torres in Mexico. He enters Nicaragua in December.

1966 He continues his studies of Ruben Dario.

He meets with Rigoberto Cruz, Silvio Mayorga, Oscar Turcios, Jose Benito Escobar, Daniel and Humberto Ortega, Enrique Lorente and Carlos Reyna. In this period work is intensified in the neighborhoods of Managua, the student movement is strengthened, work in the countryside is initiated, and the decision is made to make the necessary preparation for the implementation of armed struggle in the city and in the country. In June he journeys to the mountains to develop work aimed at establishing a guerrilla base.

On November 24 his son Carlos is born in Leon.

He stays in the mountainside until the end of August.

1967 On January 22, an anti-Somoza demonstration is organized by the bourgeois opposition, the National Opposition Union (UNO) and supported by the PSN. 60,000 heed the call and the National Guard responds by killing 400.

Fonseca signs a communique with Oscar Turcios, Rigoberto Cruz and Doris Tijerino in which the FSLN condemns the massacre, denounces the "provacateurs" of the UNO and breaks completely with the traditional left. In April he goes to the mountains in the Quirague zone with a guerrilla group. On August 6, they take on henchmen from the El Bijague region who have informed the National Guard of the guerrilla presence. As a result of detecting Sandinist guerrillas in the mountains, a bloody repression is unleashed on the peasants, torturing then killing at least ten people, including the Sandinist messenger Armando Flores. One of the three guerrilla columns is detected and destroyed at Pancasan; on August 27 Silvio Mayorga, Rigoberto Cruz, Francisco Moreno, Otto Casco, Fausto Garcia, Carlos Reyna, Ernesto Fernandez, Danilo Rosales, Carlos Tinoco and Nicolas Sanchez are killed in combat.

He arrives in Matagalpa and goes to the house of Monsignor Octavio Calderon y Padilla so that he can take him out of the city, where he remains for the week of October 8-14. On the 16th, he heads a meeting with Oscar Turcios, Tomas Borge and Daniel Ortega in a deserted house on the property of Bayardo Quintanilla. On November 16 he is transferred to the house of Lesbia Carrasquilla de Sanchez. He signs the FSLN communique on the assassinations of Sandinist militants Casimiro Sotelo, Roberto Amaya, Hugo Mendina and Edmundo Perez on November 27.

1968   On January 17 he is recognized on a national level as political and military leader of the FSLN. He directs Julio Buitrago, Ricardo Morales Aviles and other cadre as part of the reorganization of the FSLN after the losses in Pancasan. In April he writes "The Message of the FSLN to Student Revolutionaries." On May 1 he sends a message to Nicaraguan mothers: "Permit me to evoke the image of my own mother, my proletarian mother, whose days on this earth are already over. In her humility she came to understand and say with satisfaction that this is a son that belonged to his country. The memory of my mother accompanies me and nourishes me in battle. . . To all mothers of martyrs, we say: One day freedom will begin to shine forever on Nicaraguan land. That sacred freedom has its roots in your wombs." In July and August he reappears in Matagalpa and surrounding areas, with Tomas Borge and Oscar Turcios.

1969   On January 29 his daughter Tania is born. He writes *Nicaragua: Zero Hour* and on February 28, a "Brief on the Revolutionary Process in Nicaragua." The National Sandinista Liberation Front (FSLN) consolidates itself politically and ideologically, in spite of its military setbacks. He sends messages, in the organization's name: "For a victorious and guerrilla May 1st," for the 10th anniversary of the Leon student massacre of July 23, another on July 17 in homage to the fall of Julio Buitrago called, "With the blood of our martyrs we will shape a joyful future," another on August 15 after the fall of comandante Buitrago and comrades Marcos Rivera, Anibal Castrillo and Alesio Blandon, and a fifth on August 28 on guerrilla fraternity.

On August 31 he is captured in a house in Alejuela, Costa Rica.

On December 31 an attempt to rescue him from his cell in Alajuela, Costa Rica, is made by Humberto Ortega, Rufo Marin, German Pomares, Julian Roque, Fabian Rodriquez, and other Sandinist militants. The action fails: Humberto Ortega and Rufo Marin are badly wounded and are taken prisoner, along with Maria Haydee Teran de Fonseca.

1970   French intellectuals, led by Jean Paul Sartre and Simone de Beauvoir, plead for Fonseca's life and his immediate release.

He reads a lot, including Nicaraguan literature — Manolo Cuadra, Ernesto Cardenal, Sergio Ramirez.

An FSLN commando directed by Carlos Aquero succeeds for the first time in the organization's history in liberating prisoners through hostage exchanges. On October 21 Carlos Fonseca, Humberto Ortega and Rufo Marin are freed. They are sent to

Mexico and from there to Cuba. From Havana on November 7 he sends a "Message to the Nicaraguan People."

1971   In Cuba he writes various works, among them "Towards a Correct Mass Line." On October 1 he publishes a succinct history of the FSLN in *Bohemia*. He trains in North Korea along with Carlos Aguero and Rufo Marin.

1972   He lives and works in Havana on internal work of the FSLN and in March he commemorates the 38th anniversary of the assassination of Sandino with a "Brief on the Secular Intervention of North America in Nicaragua." He dedicates himself to studying the history of the country and on theoretical works. On June 28 he writes "Notes on the will of Rigoberto Lopez Perez," and in September, "Sandino: Proletarian Guerrilla."

1973   On April 10 he writes to Ernesto Cardenal about Cardenal's book *In Cuba*. In September, in Cuba he studies and has many discussions with Sandinista militants. Meanwhile the Somoza government officially announces the death of Carlos Fonseca in the clash with the National Guard in Nandaime.

1974   No information available.

1975   In August he is once more in Nicaragua. In November he writes "Synthesis of some contemporary problems." Then he integrates himself into the mountain guerrilla.

1976   He writes "Notes on the Mountain" and "Notes on Some Current Problems" in October. He is killed in combat in the Zinica region on November 7.